NOTHING PERSONAL

MONIQUE TIFFANY

authorHOUSE®

AuthorHouse™
1663 Liberty Drive
Bloomington, IN 47403
www.authorhouse.com
Phone: 1 (800) 839-8640

Published by AuthorHouse   05/16/2019

ISBN: 978-1-7283-1229-3 (sc)
ISBN: 978-1-7283-1227-9 (hc)
ISBN: 978-1-7283-1228-6 (e)

Library of Congress Control Number: 2019906822

For my mother who loved, my friends who believed, and my sister who knew. Thank you to my son and husband their never-ending support propelled me.

PROLOGUE

IT STARTED RATHER innocently. A bit cliché if you will.

"Hello. How are you?"

"I'm good. Just a bit tired."

"Would you like a lift, I could take you home."

"No thank you, maybe some other time".

Unbeknownst to them, that was the beginning of a lifelong friendship. One with benefits, mind you. The journey of two souls loving each other in spite of and despite everything destined to keep them apart, just as the frothy white tips of waves dare not stay on the sand, the games life would play with these young lovers.

After all it's just life….it's nothing personal.

CHAPTER ONE

MALCOLM WAS A young entrepreneur, destined for success and Annika was a young eighteen years old. Just out of training school and settling in her first job as a waitress.

"I have to focus on my job, no time for distractions of any form."

She was trying to convince herself.

Annika quickly settled into her new job.

Totally forgetting about that guy who offered her a lift last week. At least she tried.

She smiled.

"Maybe if I see him again I will accept the ride home." Jenna broke her chain of thought

"No sah Annika, a weh suh much people come from?"

"I just hope we get a lot of reservations this week"

"Yuh no easy, not because yuh no have a life. Hello"

The area was quite busy with tourists. Some came for vaction, some for some rest and relaxation or whatever else made their boats float.

"Jenna....don't you have anything to do?"

"Yes, miss speaky spokey.... relax man, how yuh so uptight. cho "dats why yuh no have no man."

"Whatever Jenna."

Annika went down the staircase to pick up the napkins for ironing, there standing at the foot of the stairs was Malcolm.

She was startled but played it cool. "We do not open until 6pm."

"I know that, I only came by to see you."

"Why would you do that? you don't know me."

"That's the point, I need to get to know you."

"That's not necessary. Have a good day". With that, she continued on her way.

"Are you always this cold?"

"What do you want from me, how did you get in here?"

"Your number, the door was open." He gave her a wicked smile. She looked away. He touched her hand.

"Excuse me, I have work to do."

She left him standing.

He just stared at her tight ass as she walked away from him. She was petite, about 5"4 and she was just neat. He couldn't find a better word. Neat. Yes. That was it. He had to have her. He walked away but vowed to come back later. He smiled to himself. Cold hand, warm heart.

Two weeks had passed……. she was still on his mind.

CHAPTER TWO

"**L**ukie, you should see her eyes, they close when she smiles, her laugh.... have mercy, am I going soft?"

Lukie was Malcolm's friend from law school.

"You know what makes her so fucking hot, she doesn't know how fine she is."

"Aaright Mali, so yuh a tell mi she, after two weeks, yuh know weh she live, weh she work and you know har perfume. Japanese cherry tree. Yuh a stalker now."

"Japanese cherry blossom, Luke, Jesus man."

They both laughed and continued talking.

"So Mali, (Lukie's nickname for Malcolm) wha bout di mad gyal yuh have a U.W.I.?"

"Lukie, right now I don't even know, Ive been hearing so many things."

"Cool, but yuh still haffi be careful a dem gyal yah, rich bwoy like yuh… dem gyal yah see yuh as jackpot enuh,memba dat."

"Yes yuh right, but she different, mi cyaan explain it but she different, I can tell you."

"Anything yuh say yute."

"Cool, im going to her workplace later, come with me."

"Aright den, weh she works?"

"Do you remember that old brick building we use to go chill after math class in high school?"

"Yes......dem never demolish it?"

"No, they fixed it up and opened some shops on the piazza.... she works at the Black Dhalia"

The two friends went to the restaurant that evening. It was7:30 pm

"Show mi har no." Lukie chided.

"Look, she's over there with her hair in a bun."

The supervisor was walking by at the same time.

"Who is that young lady by the booth?"

That is Annika, she is awesome, everyone wants to sit in her section."

"Ok. thank you."

"Well she looks dam good, aright den. If a she a she."

"Respect my yute."

It was 7:30 pm and service at the Black Dhalia was in full swing. Annika had pushed the encounter with Malcolm to the back of her mind.

It was service that she prided herself on giving her customers.

That was her advantage over the other servers. She was committed to ensuring that her guests had an excellent experience. She had two tables. These were patrons who had actually dined at the Black Dhalia and had enjoyed their experience so much that the place just became their spot and her, their favorite server.

"She skillfully takes our orders and serves our cocktails and appetizers without missing a beat."

"Yes, and that smile.... she is so pleasant all the time, she is getting a big tip tonight"

She was at the bar folding juice napkins while waiting for her order to be completed by the bartender. She thought someone was watching her. Correction, she felt someone watching her. She was right. Malcolm was standing to the right of the bar sipping a sex on the beach. He smiled at her. He wasn't alone. She looked away. He used that opportunity to walk over to her.

"Hi"

"I'm working, you can't be here."

"I need your number."

"I'm working."

"You are waiting. I need your number."

"You are gonna get me in trouble."

"Ok, give me a kiss then, or I'm not going to leave."

"What is wrong with you."

He began moving closer to her. She tried to move her hand, but he held on to her. She felt warm and tingly all over. She was intent on not letting it show.

"The number is…she gasped 945 8861; please I have to go, I`m busy." She hurriedly took the cocktails from the bartender and left the bar. Malcolm was smiling. He was getting through to her. Or at least that's what he thought

CHAPTER THREE

ANNIKA GREW UP in a small community in the parish of Trelawny, however her mother moved to St. James when she started high school. The first two years of high school were not very easy as her mother did not have a steady job and her father treated her and her sister as if they did not exist. Through it all. She stayed focused and did her best in school. Partly because her mother was always telling her that education was her only way out and she did not want. Annika to end up like her. Her mother, Peggy was a mother at age fourteen shortly after, her father left for the USA. He never came back.

The fact that Peggy never went to high school made things very difficult as she could not hold a steady job. She however did all she could for her Annika. Seeing this, Annika vowed to herself that she would never be made to feel dependent on anyone and she would do her best in school and she would not get caught up in the issues that she saw the young girls in her community get caught up in. Like teenage pregnancy, drug use and prostitution. Annika was a smart girl. Her mother knew that and that was going to be her way out. She was proud of Annika. High school was no challenge for Annika. She took everything in stride. She especially enjoyed her food and nutrition classes. She was a natural in the kitchen and this was where her journey into the hospitality sector began. She was encouraged by her food and nutrition teacher to continue in the field, as she thought Annika would truly excel.

After graduating high Aschool, Annika went to the local training center as her mother was not able to send her to college as she so desperately wanted. Annika was not happy about the situation, but she made the most of it. She did very well over the course of her program which was yearlong. Exactly one day after her graduation her trainer called and told Annika that she had found a job for her. She never even did an interview. She reported for work the very next day at 3pm. She met the manager, her supervisor and other workers.

The manager and Annika went over duties, shift pay among other things. She got to work at once. She was told to starch and fold the napkins which she happily obliged. She actually enjoyed doing it.

CHAPTER FOUR

IT WAS WHILE she was taking the napkins off the line at the side of the restaurant that she had caught the eyes of Malcolm whose office was adjacent to the restaurant. She had dark skin, her hair was in a bun and her uniform was immaculate. She had an aura that oozed sexuality. She was very poised, even as she took the linen from the line. She awoke something in him that had been asleep for a long time. A yearning. A desire. A thirst. He wanted her. No. He needed her.

A week after the encounter, Malcolm was still trying to understand why it was that this beautiful, poised, smart young woman couldn't see that he was interested in her.

"Damn…. Annika, even her name was sexy." He whispered to himself.

He had learned her name from the ever eager to please Jenna. He had brought lunch and flowers for her one afternoon only to find that it was her day off. He had gone to the door where he ran into her two weeks before. He sat in the waiting area that was provided for patrons of the hotel to actually sit and wait until their table was ready. After a few minutes he saw Jenna come down the stairs.

"Whoiieee, a mi yuh cyar flowers fah?"

"Hello Jenna, is the new employee here, you know, the slim…"

"Pretty black one weh yuh a look and she nuh want yuh? she name Annika, she nuh deh yah, is har day off" Jenna finished his sentence.

"Did you say it is her day off? I did not know that."

"Oh, so yuh no have har number...haha no sah dis comin like movie."

"So ahhm, so wah yuh go do wid di food? Di flowers dem pretty sah."

"Jenna, I'm not in the mood."

"But yuh no easy, a no me mek she nuh waan yuh." She hissed her teeth and walked away. she mumbled under her breath, "suit yuhself, yuh lucky."

Jenna was a busybody. Nice girl but too loud, too fake and too nosey. She had tried to get him to like her, but she just wasn't his cup of tea, he especially hated the fact that she just talked too much. How could he use that to his advantage? Annika had only given him the number to the restaurant. Not her number so he had no way of contacting her and since that evening she has been avoiding him like the plague.

He ran back to the restaurant. At the expense of lunch and flowers he emerged five minutes later with Annika's cell and home number along with her email address. Not bad, he smiled.

CHAPTER FIVE

"Why am I thinking about this young man?"

He was trouble, if she knew what was good for her she would stay far from him. Yeah right. She was constantly thinking about his smile, so refreshing.

"He is very different than any guy I had ever met."

"His grooming is impeccable, his skin so soft when he touched my hand."

She found herself wanting to taste his lips, so full and sensual.

She had to stop her mind from running wild.

Earlier that day she had received a call from Jenna saying that her boyfriend had brought her lunch and flowers, but she took them because she wasn't there. Unbeknownst to Malcolm, was the fact that Annika had told Jenna to give him the number if he asked. She did like him. Maybe he wasn't so bad after all. She would approach the situation with caution.

Malcolm was told by Jenna that Annika tutored children on her days off.

"She teach dem but she buy the tings dem wah she want from her own pocket.... book, pencil things like dat." "Mi no know how she do it."

"Do you think she will accept some supplies from me, you know supplies for the children?"

"Dats all yuh waan supply her" Jenna asked with a wide smile on her face.

"Jesus Jenna, what is wrong with you?"

"You don't fool me one-bit Malcolm…not one bit, stay deh."

"Well thanks anyway Jenna, have a good afternoon."

"Hmmm huh"

Armed with Annika's address, he was on his way.

"Annika, I am on my way to you right now." He said in a teasing tone.

"How did you get my number, she feigned surprise!"

"Jenna!"

"Ok, I guess it's alright"

"I just love the sound of her voice, so velvety smooth and sexy on the phone." He smarted.

Malcolm was soaking in ever thing about her. Ms. Peggy had heard the exchange.

"I like to see my girl smiling."

Jenna looked at her mother.

"What mommy?" she smiled.

"Nutten"

"A friend is coming over ok mommy?"

"Which fren dat? only Jenna mi know bout"

"This is a new friend mommy, please behave ok."

"aaright"

Malcolm found the house.

"Im at your gate Annika.", he had called to say. "let me in."

She smiled in her mother's direction and opened the large wrought Iron electric gate. It slid slowly from one end to the other revealing a beautifully kept yard, various fruit trees and wonderful flowers.

"Wow, a modest but beautiful home."

The driveway stretched from the gateway all the way to the garage. He was impressed.

He got out of his blue Land Rover, went to the trunk of the car and got the huge box out.

Ms. Peggy and Annika walked toward him.

"So, this must be that guy who called earlier, he is so handsome, nice car." Ms. Peggy thought.

"Hi mommy" Malcolm said as he put the box down and hugged Ms. Peggy. She smiled

"Hi Sweetie", he said to Annika. She burst out laughing.

"What are you up to Malcolm, what is in the box?"

"Just some things I thought you might need."

"Ok, thank you, what`s in it."

"Stationery for the children you tutor."

She rolled her eyes. "Jenna"

"Yup" said Malcolm.

All three of them burst out laughing.

"Ok Malcolm nice to meet you, don't be a stranger." Ms. Peggy said. She went back into the house.

"See Annika, even your mother likes me."

She turned around but her mother had gone back into the house. Ok, I will go out with you Malcolm, help me take the box inside.

He obliged. She led him into the house, through the garage where her mother was searching for something.

"Would you like something to drink Malcolm? "Yes please." He replied.

"Mommy, Malcolm and I are going out for a while is that ok?"

"This way, the fridge is over there help yourself., yes Annika"

Annika was still planted in the spot she stood. What just happened!

Her mother and Malcolm had started chatting and laughing like they had known each other a long time.

She smiled. "O well."

Malcolm and Ms. Peggy were getting along quite fine. Annika was up in her room getting ready. They were still conversing and laughing as if they were old friends.

"What would come of this." she wondered.

CHAPTER SIX

THE EVENING BEGAN with them going to see Fifty Shades of grey funny enough he was thinking that he wanted to do nasty things to her. Annika incidentally was wishing that it was her and Malcolm carrying on like that. Her panties were wet. She however pretended to not be too interested. She left the movie vowing to never take part in S and M. Malcolm only smiled at her rebuke. After the movie they went to dinner at the yacht club.

They took a table close to the water, they placed their orders and chatted about nothing in particular. Shortly, their dinner arrived at the table. She had ordered the surf and turf and he the lobster medallion it was so sensual the way she ate, without messing up her lip gloss. Her makeup almost non- existent. She was beautiful and she didn't even think about it. He couldn't take his eyes off her. They left well after 11pm. Annika enjoyed the time spent with Malcolm and he was quite the gentleman. He liked the fact that she wasn't loud or overly talkative. She smiled when Malcolm leaned over to whisper in her ear. The evening went well, and he found himself wanting more and more nights like this one. But he wouldn't rush her. He would allow her to come around on her own time.

On the ride to her house they spoke about her childhood. His college days and just about everything in between. He however left out the part about him having a fiancé. Truth be told. It was long over between them.

Malcolm had found out that she was less than faithful since she went off to university.

Ms. Peggy was on the verandah when they got home. She opened the gate and Malcolm drove in. He got out and went to open her door.

He walked her to the door. "Good evening."

Ms. Peggy smiled at him and went inside. Malcolm hugged Annika and thanked her for coming out with him, she smiled. It's not like you gave me an option. He touched her face. Goodnight my darling, Good night Malcolm. Ms. Peggy saw the exchange from the curtains and smiled.

Annika seemed so happy. If only she would let someone in her life instead of being stone cold. In essence, it was her own fault. She never spoke good about Annika's father and she generally stayed away from men. She worked hard for everything she had. Malcolm better not break her daughter's heart. Annika and her mother stayed up until the wee hours of the morning talking and drinking tea. Annika told her about her about her evening with Malcolm. She left out no detail and she was smiling all the while telling her mother about it.

"So, is he your boyfriend?"

"No. But he wants to be. I'm in no rush to have a boyfriend mom."

"I went through the stuff he brought his evening brought. I must say you will find them useful, he brought quite the variety." Said Ms. Peggy.

"Mom." Annika said, "He seems very nice, but I can't just up and fall in love with him."

"I don't know anything about him other than the fact that he is very persistent and kind."

"Jenna says he is a catch and I would be foolish not to give him a chance in my life."

"Jenna is very street-smart mommy."

"Jenna! My, that girl is something else."

"I hope you don't plan to bring her back here. Blasted feisty. I don't really want you to be friends with her. She is loud and I don't want people to think you are the same as her."

"Meaning, smart, rich, confident......?"

"Don't start."

About 3am, They both went to bed. Annika's room was upstairs. Her mother preferred to stay on the ground floor. Annika checked her phone. It was in her bag on vibrate. She saw 4 missed calls. They were all from Malcolm.

CHAPTER SEVEN

THAT NIGHT ANNIKA slept peacefully. She thought about what it might be like to be his girlfriend but then again, she thought about her mother`s words. She would give Malcolm an answer tomorrow. It felt surreal that Annika actually went out with him. She was so graceful and attractive. She had worn skin tight jeans and a loose-fitting T-shirt, butterfly ear knobs and a matching necklace that fell between her pert tits. She wore a subtle fragrance.

He had held her hand after dinner and noticed how warm she was, he kissed her fingers, she quickly pulled away her hand. It seemed he had an effect on her. He had called her when he got home but it went to voicemail. Maybe she was in the bathroom. Or already fell asleep. He was going to surprise her tomorrow. He wanted to be with her every waking hour. He wanted to be her everything. He wanted all of her. He set his alarm and closed his eyes.

She came into his room, wearing one of his white shirts. Her hair was shoulder length, black and shiny. Her nipples were firm, he could see the outline of her breasts. Damn, he was getting a hard on just looking at her she had smooth skin and shapely legs. She was not wearing panties and the t shirt barely covered her sexy ass. He could just get lost looking at her.

She walked over to him, he touched her face, his hands seem to take on a life of their own and wherever they went his lips followed. Her neck, her ears his tongue trailed along her collar bone, his fingers found her nipples. He stopped touching her, he looked into her eyes.

"I am going to take the shirt off, is that ok?"

She shook her head, afraid to speak. God, her body was blazing. He cupped her breast with both hands and let his tongue dance with her nipples he took a nipple in his mouth and sucked on it like a baby would his mother. She bit her lower lip. She felt so much pleasure. He was kissing on her body, she felt weak. Malcolm took her hand and led her to the window that opened onto a rose garden, the scent from the roses were heavenly.

He let her face the garden, palms pressed onto the tempered glass, he spread her legs. He knelt in front of her he kissed her navel then he went to her vagina, he kissed and gently nibbled on her clitoris. She nearly fell forward. He kept on sliding his tongue into her, then he would gently flick his tongue. She gasped for air.

Malcolm stopped. "I want you Annika, do you want me to fuck you?"

"You have to say yes or else I will not do it". He said throatily.

All the time he kept fingering her tight wet juicy pussy.

"Annika do you want me?"

Annika looked deep into his eyes," yes Malcolm I want you to fuck me now"

He turned her around so that her face was pressed up against the window. He thrust his already hard cock into her pussy. "O fuck, O god, you feel so good on my cock baby girl, I want you Annika." He felt his body reacting to her movements and just as he was about to cum, the phone rang.... He woke up.

CHAPTER EIGHT

MALCOLM HAD TOLD his parents about Annika. Naturally they wanted to meet her. They were pretty excited to meet anyone but that Lisette girl he had brought home a few years ago. They wanted him to date a normal girl.

"Good, we can have a pool party to welcome her, we need tiki torches, caterers, music to the invites"

"Slow down Jules, I know you are excited, but do we have time for a party" Jules was his dad`s nicknames for his wife Julia.

'We sure do." We don't need to go out every weekend, we can spend this Sunday home with the family, I`ll start making the phone calls"

And that she did just that.

"Ok. Then" said Malcolm and his dad in unison, they started laughing. Once Julia got something on her mind she would do it.

"Are you in the mood for a drink son?"

"Yes, dad we need it"

"Michael honey, bring me scotch neat"

"Sure love."

Malcolm called Annika that night to let her about the plans for a party on Sunday.

"I will come and pick you up on Sunday, say around 11am."

"Ok. I'll be waiting."

"Wear something sexy."

She smiled

"By the way, you can have Jenna tag along."

She laughed," If you insist".

Jenna was at Annika's house early that Sunday morning chatting and laughing and irritating Ms. Peggy.

"So, girl how much tip yuh mek lastnight? me notice say yuh people dem no siddung wid nobody else when dem come a di restaurant"

"Your people don't sit with anyone else either so what are you talking about, how much did you make?"

"Me make seven grand last night."

"That's nice, I made eight thousand two hundred. That goes in the bank first thing in the morning."

"Gyal yuh save every dollar yuh make, yuh too good".

"Jenna, I told you I am going to college as soon as I save up enough money, what do you do with your money? Pardon me not everyone is rich like you."

"Rich no has nutten to do with it. I save too, plus you have Malcolm who will give you anything if yuh ask."

"I will not ask for a handout, I am fine. I don't understand you, your parents a wealthy and you just waste your time being a spoilt brat. Do you ever think about your future Jenna?"

"Nope"

"Why the hell would you, your children's children will never want for anything, I on the other hand have to work for everything I want, and I honestly don't mind so that's why I save."

"Relax Miss speaky spokey, calm down I understand, give me a hug"

"you are my best and only friend, but you drive me crazy"

"If I don't who will" Jenna and Annika laughed

The girls were as different as any two people could be, but they were friends. Jenna's parents were old money, the Jameson family even owned slaves back in the old days. Jenna didn't have to worry about anything.

If the world turned upside down, she would still be ok. she preferred being unruly and she hated speaking English. You wouldn't know she was born in England.

Her mother despised her working as a waitress, so Jenna thoroughly enjoyed her mother's misery. Her dad loved his rebellious daughter. He would move heaven and earth to keep her smiling. Jenna came home with red hair one day in the sixth grade. She had had long, thick black hair. Her mother had a fit.

When asked what happened Jenna had replied,

"I saw the color and I loved it, so I had the driver pay to do it."

That was the beginning of it all. She was a good child nonetheless. Her family loved her.

Malcolm came to pick the girls up at 10:45am.

They kissed Ms. Peggy goodbye and was on their way.

"Drive safely." she shouted after them.

CHAPTER NINE

THE HOUSE SAT on a hill overlooking the community of Ironshore. The gates were flanked by two enormous lifelike lions sitting on Grecian style columns on either side. Sprawling well-manicured lawns.

"This is beautiful", Annika said

Jenna broke the spell." So, what your parents do, sell drugs"

Annika shot her a wicked stare. Jenna herself lived in a very big house.

She laughed because she knew exactly what her friend was thinking.

"Well if you must know Jenna"

"Yes, mi need fi know because yuh and mi fren deh and if anything, happen to her mi need fi know wha fi tell di police bout yuh and yuh family" she interrupted.

The stare came again.

"As I was saying, my father is a lawyer and my mother is a psychiatrist. Both very successful. I also have a sister who is a judge in London".

"So, a yuh alone no come out to nutten" Jenna stated matter of factly.

"Shut up Jenna"

"Jenna, I swear, I don't know what to do with you" Malcolm said as they all started laughing.

"Welcome to my humble abode ladies"

The car pulled into a four-car garage. Malcolm ushered the girls into the house. through the kitchen and onto the back patio and pool deck.

"Jenna please behave" Malcolm was practically pleading.

She stuck out her tongue.

"Here they are. Hope the journey wasn't too long, it's great to have you, Annika and Jenna I presume."

"O Annika you sure are beautiful."

"Thank you, Annika," replied

Jenna, I have heard a lot about you"

"Like what?" Jenna asked

"Wow mom how did you get all these people here, Malcolm quickly changed the subject

"Vera Wang certainly looks good on you Mrs. Jervais"

"Thank you, Jenna, how did you know, and I think its best you call me Julia"

"I just do" she smiled.

"Trust me Mrs. Jervais, she is a fashionista don't be fooled."

"Didn't know you spoke English Malcolm teased"

"Fuck off"

"Mrs. Jervais heard the exchange. She liked Jenna."

She led them to the bar.

"Malcolm get these ladies something to drink, will you?"

She took Annika by the hand. "Your friend has a very colorful personality, doesn't she?" They smiled at each other. "You my love are perfect for Malcolm, we have heard so much about you. It's so good to finally see you in person"

"Thank you, I am happy to hear you say that, I must say I was pretty nervous about meeting you today"

"No need to be my love, we are quite normal regardless of what you have heard." This from a deep voice with an English accent.

He kissed he wife on the lips.

He hugged Annika.

"I do hope you ladies are enjoying the party".

"Well, I can see why Malcolm is head over heels with you, you are lovely"

"Thank you, sir,"

"Jules, did she just call me sir?"

Julia was laughing." Yes honey, she did."

"Annika" she said while still laughing, "He really doesn't like being called sir, it makes him feel old." She was laughing so hard she started tearing up.

Annika couldn't help but laugh too.

They were still recovering from laughter when Malcolm and Jenna came back with a drink for them all.

"What is so funny?" She asked

"I called Mr. Jervais sir" Annika laughed.

"Let's face it dad, you are getting there." They all started laughing again.

"Hi, I'm Jenna Jameson", no relation to the pornstar.

Michael looked Jenna in the eye. "Nice to meet you Jenna, no relation to the pornstar."

"She is a firecracker Michael, be careful"

"Well it's a good thing it's a pool party, let's go mingle"

Malcolm held Annika around the waste and pulled her close to him.

"I love you Annika," He kissed her lips.

They all walked toward the other people at the party, introducing the girls to everyone.

The music was playing, and the sun was shining down. It was a beautiful day.

"I am happy. I love Malcolm and I feel like his parents do like me. I can see myself here with these people for the rest of my life. I truly am happy." Annika's thoughts were running away with her. She was happy.

CHAPTER TEN

"Annika is very beautiful, she reminds me of you when we first met, she has that same light in her eyes."

"O stop." Julia said.

"I know you see it too."

"Yes hon, I do see it, she is a strong one."

Our son sure is smitten by her. He smiles everytime he looks at her, he is always holding her hand."

"That is more than I can say for the gold digger Lisette: I sure never liked her."

"No, you did not my love, you didn't."

By this time Malcolm and the girls were upstairs, he had given them a tour of the house and they were now in one of the guest's rooms.

This room was like walking out into a meadow. So open and breezy and it looked out onto the Caribbean Sea.

"O the view, everything is white and chic if I say so myself" Jenna was already jumping on the huge bed.

"Yup, my mother decorated."

"There are two bags in the closet for you girls, get comfy and meet me by the pool ok."

He kissed Annika" I love you babe."

He gave Jenna the finger as he stepped out the door.

"Sit on it"

"So why yuh so quiet miss Jenna said to her friend"

"Nothing just thinking."

"Think about what"

"Everything."

"Well his family seems very nice"

"Yeah especially daddy." Jenna smirked

"Wah inna dem bag yah, watch yah girl, bathsuit towel, slippers and shades."

They are from his mom

"Wow them look good, brand to."

"Have mercy girl, as I was saying, his parents seem nice. The house is amazing."

"Malcolm serious about yuh enuh." "Imagine dem throw big party fi yuh, den imagine when oonuh married."

"Well I must say I was surprised"

"Yasss girl, nice life fi wi"

Both girls began laughing while getting dressed for the pool.

Luke got there a few minutes ago. He was at the bar. Both men had cold beers in their hands. They were laughing and talking.

Luke turned around just as they the girls were coming down the stairway.

"Wow who are those hotties?"

"My girl and her friend." Malcolm stated matter of factly.

"Fi real, wow so who dat beside har?"

"Jenna"

"Yuh too lie, a so she looks good outta her uniform.

"I guess."

"Her body loud up tho."

"Hey ladies" Malcolm waved them over

"Nuh da same bwoi deh Malcolm did bring a di restaurant?".

"Yes, Jenna that is Luke and he is looking at you."

"Him can no bother mi naah look nobody"

They both waved back.

26

CHAPTER ELEVEN

THE WEEKEND WENT by so quickly. It was a great trip and it turned out to be very special to them both. Malcolm had parked in the Harbor View.

He was now on his way to pick up his vehicle. Annika was very happy and that made him happy. Ms. Peggy called every evening at six to check on her daughter. Hearing how happy she sounded made her content. His phone was ringing now, that familiar ring of the iPhone. It could only be one person.

"Really", Malcolm said under his breath......... "at this very moment?".

He declined the call. What he really wanted to do was to turn the phone off. He decided against it. The phone started to ring again while on the Norman Manley Highway. He was holding hands with Annika.

"Shit" he thought.

how the hell was he going to deal with this at this moment. Malcolm knew she wouldn't stop calling if she didn't get through to him. He may as well not delay the inevitable.

"Hello Darling" came the high pitched, excited voice.

. "Hi, ahmm". How are you? He tried to sound normal.

"I'm great honey, I miss you. I called to tell you that I may come home by tonight or tomorrow......... hello...........Malcolm...........hello."

CHAPTER TWELVE

ANNIKA WAS LYING in bed thinking about yesterday on the drive down from Port Royal. Malcolm had received a phone call; the conversation wasn't clear, but she was certain that it was a woman.

It wasn't Malcolm's mom because she always spoke to Annika first, then him. What perplexed her was the way he was antsy after that.

He became irritable and far off in thinking, he barely spoke to her and when he did, it was from being polite. She had asked who it was and he brushed it off as nothing important. He went as far as to put his phone on vibrate in his pocket.

She did not know what it was, but she knew something was amiss.

Malcolm had dropped her off and barely spent half an hour at her house, he said he had to sort something out by the office. He did not ask her if she wanted to come along as he normally would.

"O well. I guess if he wanted to talk about it he would", She forced the thought out of her mind and went to her mom's room to chat about the events of the weekend retreat. Something made her not tell her mother about the phone call.

"Annika, you seem restless what is troubling you child." said her mom.

"Nothing mother" Ms. Peggy knew she was lying but decided not to push her, she would come to her in time.

CHAPTER THIRTEEN

IT WAS ABOUT 8:15pm, on Tuesday, there was an uneasy look on Malcolm`s face. He would flinch each time a headlight shone in his direction. Every time his phone rang. He had been flustered ever since he got that phone call from Lisette.

He had some whiskey, straight from the bottle, swig after swig. He finally decided to go shower. He laid on his bed, but sleep was eluding him.

After going over the happenings of the weekend and how he hadn't gone to Annika`s house to see if she was alright. He knew he was being distant but right now he had a lot on his mind. Seeing Annika now wouldn't make him feel any better, at least that's what he thought. He finally drifted off to sleep.

Not even two hours after, there was a knock at the door, Malcolm thought he was dreaming so he ignored the sound by putting a pillow over his head.

The knock never ceased…. He finally got up, went down the stairs and still groggy from sleeping he opened the door, it was Lisette, all smiles and a s bubbly as ever. "My God" Malcolm thought to himself.

"Hi honey", she shrieked, "Surprise", she kissed him on the lips right then in the doorway then walked past him into the house. He stood there trying to take it all in, "What have I gotten myself into"?

Annika hadn't heard from Malcolm in a few days. That is except for the basic text message. She was a bit worried about him, especially since that weird phone call that had him acting all strange since their return from the retreat. She had fallen in love with Malcolm against her better judgement. She really cared about him. Now she was busy second guessing herself.

"Did I fall in love too fast, was he playing me....... I can't believe I let him play me like a fool." The tears welled in her eyes. She excused herself from her mother's room.

Jenna had realized that her friend hadn't been herself and she had decided to speak to her after their shift but seeing her in tears made her decide not to wait. Something had happened to make Annika behave in this fashion and she would get to the bottom of it.

"Annika, from yuh come back yuh deh act strange, wah do yuh?"

Annika looked at Jenna and feigned a happy face.

"What do you mean?"

"Annika, everybody notices how you look stress a bet a da bwoy deh, Annika wah do yuh?"

Annika knew that Jenna would not stop until she was pleased and it made no sense delaying the inevitable.

"I haven't heard from Malcolm in two days."

"So yuh no know weh him live?"

"Yes, but ......"

"But nothing" Jenna said, "go over there...yuh no easy, before yuh go see wah deh tek place, yuh deh yah deh bawl."

Annika had never thought of going over to Malcolm's house, he was always coming to her house, she had thought nothing of it. Not until these past days.

"Should I go over to his house", She wondered, Annika left work that night with many thoughts going through her mind.

She tried calling him, but the phone went to the voicemail. She and Jenna were walking to the parking lot asked her again "Do you want me to come with you? She thought about it for a minute.

"Yes, Jenna let`s go."

"Ok. Let`s go." Jenna took her keys from her pocket. She hurried Annika along. The girls headed in the direction of Malcolm`s house.

CHAPTER FOURTEEN

THEY GOT TO the house at around 11pm.

They pulled over on the sidewalk just before they got to his gate. The girls literally sneaked into the yard and around to the side where there was a large window that took up a whole side of a wall. They both peered through the thin brown curtains at first, they saw nothing, if it wasn't for the car in the driveway, they would have thought he wasn't home. They heard laughter, the both ducked their heads when he walked into the room. He looked haggard. He sat on a black leather chair. He just sat there. A few minutes had passed, and the girls were just about ready to leave thinking that nothing was amiss, when a petite, light skinned female sauntered into the room naked. She straddled Malcolm. Malcolm tried easing her off him. She started kissing his face, his lips.

Annika let out a scream that shrilled through the quiet night air.

CHAPTER FIFTEEN

MS. PEGGY WAS beside herself with worry. Annika had not left her room, she hadn't eaten since the night before. What was worse, she was silent. Malcolm had come by, but Annika did not see him or even seemed interested to speak to him. Jenna had stayed until morning. Something was not right.

Annika had not told her mother about the previous night. She did not know that Malcolm came over the very same night. Malcolm had run out of the house upon hearing the scream, he knew instantly that it was Annika. He had spotted Jenna's car pulling away from his gate.

He knew that his secret was blown. How dumb of him to not see this coming. Lisette wasn't the least bit perturbed by the scream. She had heard it and wondered why Malcolm had been so surprised. He had driven over to the house, but Jenna would not let him in, and it was too late to wake Ms. Peggy. He kept calling Annika but that had proven futile. He had decided to come by in the morning. He drove home that night vowing to fix this mess he had created.

It was obvious that something was not right between Annika and Malcolm, but nothing was being said by either of them. She could only wait until her daughter was ready to talk.

Jenna had driven her home that night. She was there until about seven that morning. Her friend had taken It real hard and she had to be there for her. Jenna had called ahead and told their supervisor that Annika wasn't well and wound not be in for the rest of the week.

It hurt Jenna to see Annika like this. There was no way that Annika could go to work. She had been weeping uncontrollably since last night and she hadn't eaten a thing. Jenna had seen the calls from Malcolm and had went ahead and turned the phone off.

CHAPTER SIXTEEN

LISETTE DIDN'T CARE as she had her own agenda but that was her little secret. She had been involved with a final year student at the university and she was now pregnant with his child. She hadn't told him about it as she wanted to get Malcolm to father the child by having sex with him then pretend to be pregnant at the appropriate time.

Malcolm had money, he loved her, he was going to marry her. She messed up and now had to think about her life as she knew it. She didn't wish to lose all the perks that came with being Malcolm's fiancé.

She refused to be tied up with a nobody. She was just having fun. It was just unfortunate that she became pregnant.

It now seemed that Malcolm had secrets of his own, but she wasn't going to be perplexed by whatever or whoever he was involved with. She would just allow things to play out.

Thing is Malcolm and Lisette had been over for quite some time now.

"I refused to accept it, how can Malcolm move on from me? I Refuse to believe it"

Annika was beside herself. How did she allow herself to be duped? She had held out for so long and now this. The one guy she had allowed herself to fall for was now her source of heartache. She had cried enough. She consoled herself. 'It's time to get up and get on with life.

She was in her room for three days. It was now Saturday and she felt better but not completely. Every now and again a tear would escape her eye. Malcolm had kept calling and when he found out she wasn't at work, he went to her house.

She would not speak to him though. He sent her another message. All the others went either unread or she just didn't respond. This one was saying that she either make time to speak to him or he would speak to her mother. She didn't want that but she really wasn't in the mood to speak to Malcolm at this moment.

She would tell her mother and get it over with. She went to her mother's room.

"Mom, I am no longer seeing Malcolm. It didn't work out. I prefer not to talk about it. Please do not go investigating."

"ok then" her mother said, a bit startled.

Annika left the room.

Ms. Peggy would not be fooled. She knew her daughter and her daughter were heartbroken, and she loved Malcolm. You don't just get over a first love like that. Malcolm had some explaining to do.

CHAPTER SEVENTEEN

MALCOLM HAD DECIDED that the least he could do was to give Annika some time to cool off, however in the meantime, he would speak to her mother. He loved Annika and he never wished to see her hurt. At this point he didn't know what to do but he was going to try to fix things.

He understood what it all seemed like and he could not blame her for not wanting to have anything to do with him. He decided he was going over to the house after work this evening. He found out that Annika had taken a week off from work, so he knew she wasn't handling the situation well.

In the time that they had been dating, he had come to realize that even though Annika was a sweet and gentle soul, she also was headstrong in her beliefs and when she was hurting, she could not hide it. What had he done?

Jenna was treating him as though he had a bad case of leprosy. She was not hiding how she felt about him and he had no one to blame but himself. Jenna was truly a great friend to Annika and she was not in the mood to play nice with the person who hurt her friend.

Malcolm approached Jenna in the parking lot that afternoon.

"Jenna, it's not what it looked like at my house the other night"

Jenna hissed her teeth, yuh must think say we now have no sense.

"We were together, but not since I met Annika, I swear it." Malcolm pleaded. He reached out to touch Jenna's shoulder.

"Yeah whatever, the whole a oonuh a di same thing; move from side a mi a no touch mi."

"Jenna, just give me five minutes I really need to speak to you. I need you to understand."

"Mi really no inna nutten wid yuh enuh Malcolm."

"Please Jenna."

"Mi naah go stand up inna di sun wid yuh enuh."

"Ok, let's go to the pub, we can talk there."

Malcolm and Jenna sat in the pub talking for over an hour, he had explained that Lisette and himself were together and the fact that it all changed when Lisette went off to school. He had known of Lisette and her not so sweet behavior. Lisette on the other hand hadn't a clue that Malcolm was aware of her devious ways.

He told Jenna everything. For the first she was at a loss for words. She went on to tell Malcolm that he should have come clean a long time ago instead of allowing things to escalate. Malcolm agreed. He told her that he was on his way to see Ms. Peggy when he left the pub, coincidentally that was where Jenna was headed as well.

Jenna felt for Malcolm at this point. She understood how he may be feeling but her allegiance was to her friend. She decided that he wasn't too bad after hearing all that.

They both got in their cars and headed to Annika's house.

CHAPTER EIGHTEEN

ANNIKA HAD JUST stepped outside.

She sat under the tree in her yard, her favorite spot. Cool and quiet. She was going over the events of the past week. Mostly that scene at Malcolm's house. She honestly thought she saw him try to push her away.

He even seemed to be drunk. If only she could be sure. Seconds later Jenna pulled up at her gate. Opening it with the remote control she had given her, then driving up to the garage. Surprisingly, Malcolm was behind her.

Malcolm saw her sitting under the tree, she looked sad, her hair was down. He did not wish to see her sad.

He parked his car and walked towards Annika, in his mind, he willed her not to move.

She didn't.

Jenna came running up to her, Hey girl, whats up? "Why yuh siddung unda di tree wid yuh face long dung like fi donkey?"

She smiled and hugged her friend. Malcolm caught up to them.

"Hi Annika."

"Hi."

"Annika yuh and Cassanova really need fi talk, das why mi an him come. Listen to him, him chat mi out already so mi a go inside golook food." "Weh mommy deh?"

Jenna did not wait for an answer. She was already on her way inside the house.

"Annika, can I talk to you for a while. I really need you to understand some things."

"Ok Malcolm, What could you possibly have to tell me." She gave him the evil eye.

"Annika, I know it looked bad, but I assure you that her and I are way over. And we have been for a while. It's just that she caught me when I was drunk. I'm not making excuses, I really am sorry you had to see that. I tried pushing her away, but I had drunk so much earlier that much".

He went on to tell her about the affair at college, the call he had received and how sorry he was for the way he had handled the situation.

"Malcolm, why didn't you think you could tell me all this before all that transpired.?, I love you but you obviously don't love me as much as you say you do, or else you would have been honest with me from the get-go." Tears escaped her eyes.

He took her into his arms, he apologized over and over and told her he wouldn't ever hurt her again in any way.

"I'm sorry Annika, I love you and I really hope you can forgive me and give me a chance to make things right."

"Where is she now?" Annika asked.

"I honestly do not know, I left her at the house, I told her not to be there when I get back."

"Really now." Annika responded.

Malcolm had been so upset with her that he really did tell her his mind.

Annika, despite how she was feeling, let herself melt in his arms. The smell of his aftershave, his cologne. Invictus. She felt only love for this man. She did not move. She wanted to hold on to him.

She looked up at him. Deep into his eyes.

"Do you love me?"

His response was to take her face into his hands and slowly kiss her face, he kissed away her tears. He then kissed her lips ever so slowly, she kissed him back. she started to cry again.

After what seemed like an eternity, they hugged. He stood up and took her hand.

"Let's go inside" he helped her to her feet, they held hands and went inside the house.

Jenna and Ms. Peggy looked up to see the young couple hand in hand coming into the kitchen where they both were eating ice cream and talking.

"Ok, then". Ms. Peggy said, she smiled.

"Ice cream anyone?" Jenna laughed.

Malcolm kissed Annika's forehead. She rubbed his arm. She had gotten her man back. She would never let him go.

Malcolm ordered pizza and they all spent the rest of the evening playing board games and watching movies. No one was unhappy.

CHAPTER NINETEEN

LISETTE HAD BEEN calling Malcolm all evening, the call went straight to voicemail. his phone was off. She had found out that he knew of her fling with the guy at university.

The argument they had had been very intense and it had ended with Malcolm telling her to kindly leave his house. She could keep the ring, after all it was given to her when she was his world.

She knew that he was serious. She went to the bar and opened a bottle of Meomi. She poured some into a glass. Downed it and thought better of using the glass. She put the bottle to her head. The more she drank the more she cried.

She lay on the carpet and cried herself to sleep. Lisette had thought that she could somehow convince Malcolm that they could get over all this, it was no to be. He took the betrayal hard. The guy was his friend's brother. It was too close to home. He could not look at her in the same light. He had said as much.

She would go back to her parent's house in Ironshore, her parents would know what to do. They were both doctors. She would then go back to university and start a fresh.

Lisette was alone, it was her own doing.

Malcolm had done his best to fix things between him and Annika. He also apologized to both Ms. Peggy and Jenna. He was now from Lisette and could focus on the future with Annika.

Months had passed and things were really going great between the two.

Malcolm had taken a keen interest in Annika`s life and he made sure that she was taken care of. He had opened a savings account in her name and made deposits very regularly. He was also very instrumental in her acquiring visas for America, the United Kingdom and Canada. Annika had quit her job at the restaurant to pursue a degree in accounting.

She was overwhelmed with the changes that had occurred in her life directly as a result of her relationship with Malcolm. Mind you, they were all positive changes. She was happy. Her mother was happy, and Jenna was very happy to see her friend happy.

Malcolm sat at his desk looking at a photo that they had taken while in Bahamas for a short well needed vacation. He loved Annika and she loved him as well. She had never given him reason to doubt. She was a good girl, nothing like Lisette.

As he was about to dial her number, she came through the office doors.

She was wearing a light blue summer dress. It had very delicate buttons that went all the way down to her thighs. Her hair was in a bun and she wore tiny diamond studs. Her sandals were Rebecca Minkoff, as was the purse her delicate fingers held on to.

She had a way of adorning herself in simple clothing and looked like a million dollars every time. She was very beautiful and oozed sexuality. He had to tear his gaze away from her for a minute.

What a surprise my love, was just about to call you. He said, while getting up to greet her.

I decided to stop by and take you out for lunch, my treat.

He smiled, she was so full of life. He kissed her face, then her lips. She kissed him back. Malcolm gently pulled her close to him, he kissed her neck, slowly at first but turned on by the smell of her, he kissed her harder, leaving a hickey.

She smiled. You sure are happy to see me. I never thought I was going to be lunch she laughed. He lifted her onto his desk. He kissed her hard on the lips. His tongue darted around in her mouth, he knew this turned her on. She had her fingers in his hair.

"Malcolm!" she gasped.

He was now undoing her buttons, with each button he undid he placed a kiss. He let the bra strap fall off her shoulder. He toyed with her exposed nipple using his tongue and slowly took it into his mouth. She gasped. He kept at it until she was naked on his desk. He knelt before her, spread her legs.

He loved eating her pussy. The way she would cum when he did it drove him over the edge. He slid his tongue inside her.

"Oooh babe."

He was already going wild. She opened herself to him. He drove her wild with his tongue. He always made sure she was satisfied.

"Do you like that my dear?"

"You know I do baby." she whispered.

She had gotten bolder sexually and she sometimes surprised herself. She got down off the desk and started kissing him. They were now on the floor. She was naked on top of Malcolm who was still in his suit. She loosened his tie, unbuttoned his shirt and slid his pants down his ankles, he couldn't wait…. he kicked them off hurriedly.

She began stroking his cock. He was kissing her breast and using his finger to massage her pussy. Annika kissed his member, then began to make long strokes with her tongue from the base to the tip and back. Malcolm was going crazy. This felt so good. She took all of him in her mouth she was kissing and sucking and stroking his cock all at once.

Oh God baby, you are so good to me. He loosened her bun and now her hair was in his hand, he felt himself overcome with wild abandon she felt it too, she continued his torment.

He lifted her from the ground and positioned her doggy style on the desk. He plunged into her pussy, she winced, but she was enjoying it, she was grinding on his cock and he was slapping her ass and calling her name they were giving of themselves to each other and at that moment no one or nothing else mattered. He turned her face to his and kissed her, she looked into his eyes while he was fucking her, she loved him.

She was nearing climax, as was Malcolm. He held her by the waist and thrust harder. She screamed his name as she climaxed he did seconds later. They were frozen in time. They laid on the carpet in the office and kissed each other for what seemed like eternity.

They finally got up and cleaned up in the office bathroom. They stepped outside into the afternoon sun smiling at each other as if they had a secret they did not wish to share. They were happy. They walked over to his car.

Lunch was now on him.

CHAPTER TWENTY

"**A**nnika, you have to marry me................
let me finish, Annika, you have made me love you many times over...you have made me a better person than whom I was before. I want to spend my life with you, I don't see any other way about it....... you have to marry me."

Malcolm had been in the foyer pacing talking out loud to himself.... he was ready. Annika meant everything to him and he wanted to show her just what that meant. Would she give him the chance though?

He hadn't been the best he could be to her, in fact.... he had started seeing a young woman not far from his house, he had convinced himself that she was just a one-night stand and didn't mean anything. Why was he always getting himself into these situations?

It was his thinking that Annika would never leave. He thought that because he had done a lot for her, that she would just turn her pretty eyes and act as if she wasn't aware of what was happening.

Truth is.... Annika did know, she just chose her battles wisely. Her mom taught her that lesson a long time ago.

It had so happened that Jenna and Annika had gone to Scotchie`s in Discovery Bay, just to have a light lunch, listen to music and look out onto the Caribbean Sea.

They had been there for less than fifteen minutes when Annika saw her man……. Malcolm stroll in…. hand in hand with a young woman. She had seemed familiar, but Annika wasn't the type for confrontations.

The table she had chosen wasn't quite visible to everyone else, but she had the vantage point. Jenna hadn't seen Malcolm and for that, Annika was grateful. Jenna had seen her demeanor change but didn't get into it.

"Hey girl, if you aren't feeling this, we can take the food and go."

Jenna didn't even wait for a reply…. she called the waiter over and requested just that. They paid and left. Jenna and Malcolm were none the wiser.

Malcolm needed to shape up, or else Annika would pull the plug on what they had. She was content to pretend that all was well but if Malcom was taking his latest conquest out in public she definitely couldn't stand for that.

She was hurting, that night she cried until she was numb. She didn't know what to do with that feeling and she could not even talk to her mother about it. That was the worst part. She got two phone calls that night…Jenna asking what today was all about and Malcolm asking if she was alright and that he was on his away over. She quickly got up and went to take a shower.

She didn't want him to see her the way she was. Why was she always allowing him to get the best of her…? why didn't she leave as she said she would…. over and over again.

"Annika, I assure you. She didn't mean anything this will not happen again. I love you, you mean the world to me."

"I love you too, but you can't treat me like this. I deserve better."

Yes, you do, I know that. I have no excuse.

"You are lying to me as we speak."

"What do you mean? I`m not lying."

"Malcolm, I saw you today. I was at Scotchies with Jenna. I saw you walk in hand in hand what girl..." Annika began crying.

"I have never cheated on you, I have always made you proud but I guess I will never be enough for you Malcolm Jervais"

He hated to see her like this.

"Annika, I love you. That girl doesn't mean anything to me she is not even in the picture anymore. I only want you. There is no excuse. I want you alone."

"Please, please", he begged.

"Give me another chance honey. I know I fucked up, but I can fix it I promise; you know I will never leave you."

"Aren't you tired of lying? have you no heart."

"I'm fucked, how can I save us" …he knew he blew it. Malcolm took her face in his hands

"Look at me darling"

She looked in his eyes.

"I love you babygirl."

She closed her eyes

He kissed her lips. She stiffened her lips against his. He applied pressure. She opened her eyes and tears ran down her face.

"Do you not see how much I love you?"

"I love you too Annika."

"No, you don't." she shouted." You only like the idea of me."

He slid his tongue between her lips. Her body shivered.

He placed his hand at the nape of her neck. He kissed her ever so slowly. His tongue was dancing with hers. He used his free hand to outline her breast. He circled her right nipple. She tried to protest. He thrust his tongue deeper in her mouth. He now cupped her breast so firm but yet so soft.

He let go of her neck but continued kissing her. Both hands were driving her in sane. He slid his hand between her legs. The shirt she was wearing did not act as a barrier to him, in fact it made her for accessible. His finger found its way to her warmth, radiating hot heat. His tongue was now trailing her neck. Every kiss, every nibble made her melt in his arms.

"You can`t do this Malcolm"

"Why not, you belong to me." He slid the shirt from her arms. It dropped to her hips. Her breasts were now bare. He licked her boob like an infant did an ice cream cone. She was wet at this point. His fingers knew where to play. She gasped with pleasure. He gently eased her down to the carpet. He opened her legs, she tried to fight, barely. He was kissing her belly. torturing her with his tongue. He painstakingly made his way to her treasure trove.

"Malcolm." she cried out.

"Yes baby."

"Please don't"

"Don't what, this? his tongue was massaging her clit just the way she like it; or this" he gently sucked on her labia, or do you mean this baby?, he let his tongue slide over her fourchette over and over again."

"Malcolm, I can`t take this."

"But you can darling."

He slid his tongue inside her while he tickled her anus with his index finger, light as a feather. He knew she enjoyed this and he knew she would come if he continued. He loosened his pants and slid it down his legs. By this he was rock hard and wanted her so badly. He thrust his cock deep inside her. She screamed. He began to survey her vaginas warmth with his manhood. She felt so good and he wanted her every bit of her. more and more every second. He could feel her climaxing, thing is he was climaxing too he thrust harder, she screamed louder, she dug her nails deeper, he kissed her harder. Their bodies had become one with every action. They both came at the very same moment in time. Both in their own world but together as one. They were spent.

"I love you." they both said to each other in unison. The only difference was their names.

"I love you too." Again, both together.

Theirs was destiny they could not escape.

They laid there on the floor together for what seemed eternity.

"I promise I'll be better" He whispered in her ear. She was barely awake. He covered her with the blanket from off her bed, kissed her forehead. She was fast asleep when he left. He had a lot on his mind. He hadn't planned on being unfaithful to her, he just couldn't stop himself. The Jervais curse. Annika woke up in the early hours of the morning. She had heard him drive away a few hours ago.

"I need to clear my head. I need to get be alone for a while." She was thinking that she was over Malcolm, over the cheating and lies. She slid under her covers and fell asleep.

Malcolm got home and just laid out in the sofa. He felt as if he made love to Annika for the last time.

CHAPTER TWENTY-ONE

"**M**ommy, stop telling me what to do. Im not trying to be rude but I am quite fine. I needed a break from Malcolm and I took it."

"Yuh stubborn like yuh father enuh girl I don't know how yuh come so."

It was almost three weeks now that Annika went away to her aunt in St. Ann. She spoke to her mom, Jenna. She had sent Malcolm an email telling him that she was going to be away for a while. She needed to think about the relationship, her life and about where she wanted to be. She asked him to honor her request and give her space. Not that she was asking permission. She was just being civil about it.

"I'm back now so you guys can relax."

"So wah the plan now? Jenna asked".

"I second that." Came her mother.

"I don't know, I'm just going to take it one step and one day at a time."

"Before I went to St. Ann I was depressed and miserable, I was sad didn't you guys see that, what do you want me to do go back to that because of Malcolm?"

"So yuh tell him about the baby?" Ms. Peggy asked the question that stunned Jenna but made Annika look away.

"You don't think you could hide it from me girl, me a yuh mother."

She hugged her mother then. "No mommy I just didn't want to say anything yet."

"So, wait, yuh tell Malcolm yet? This time the question came from Jenna. 'He needs to know Annika."

"Yes, I know." I will tell him eventually I'm just taking it slow I just got back I don't want to just jump back into what I was running from to begin with."

"That man loves you, he has been here every day since you left, he seems to have cleaned up his act."

With that Jenna left the room. The other two women were so deep in conversation they didn't realise that she had stepped away.

"Well if she won't tell him I have to." Annika was smart and intelligent but very impulsive and she always stood by her decisions. Good or bad. Malcolm needed to know he had a child on the way.

"Hey Jenna, what's up with you?"

"Ahhm I'm good, mi need fi talk to you"

"Ok, talk I'm a bit busy here."

"This serious trust me"

"What is it?"

"Annika is back, she is pregnant"

"What, how come she didn't tell me, where are you?"

"Mi deh a har house.

"Ok I'm on my way."

Malcolm was nervous but he was happy, now she wouldn't say no. He was going to ask her to marry him. He was also angry. How could she not tell him that she was carrying his child. Was it his child? As much as he was angry, he also remembered that he was the reason she was feeling and acting the way she was, the reason she left for St. Ann. It had been almost a month, but he understood she was still hurting; thing is he never even saw that girl again. He had broken off the relationship that evening at Scotchies. Annika hadn't believed him. How could she he had lied to her countless times. He had no one to blame but himself. He arrived at the house to find Jenna and Ms. Peggy sitting under the big tree in the yard.

"Good afternoon ladies."

"Hi Malcolm, so Jenna called you, gyal yuh no easy at all."

Jenna laughed.

"Where is my girl, how is she doing?"

"She is inside sleeping on the sofa."

"Ms. Peggy, I swear I didn't know she was pregnant, I wouldn't abandon her. I loved her since the first day I laid eyes on her."

He took the ring from his pocket. Both Jenna and Ms. Peggy gasped at the diamond ring Malcolm had in his hand.

"O my lord, yuh serious bout this man."

"Yes maam, I am asking you for your daughters' hand in marriage."

Jenna had tears rolling down her face. This girl rarely if ever showed her soft side.

Malcolm hugged her.

"You have to be good to her Malcolm, you have to make her happy. You need to find a way to be a good husband to her."

"I will Jenna I promise." He knew she loved Annika and didn't want to see her hurting.

"Ok im gonna go get my woman."

Malcolm literally ran up to the house. He couldn't wait to see her it has been long enough since he held her in his arms, kissed her and now here they were, she was having his baby.

Annika was just waking up from a short nap

"Hey honey, he went over and planted a big kiss on her lips. He hugged her to his chest." How are you sweetie, how are you feeling?"

"I'm good, I missed you, believe it or not." They laughed."

"I need to tell you something Malcolm. It`s important."

He kissed her lips, "its ok honey. I know and I will never leave you ever, I love you so very much."

He went down on one knee. "I know I haven't been the best and I cannot fix the past but I can and I will work hard so you and our son will be alright."

"Son" she laughed.

"Please give me a chance to prove to you that I am the man you want. Forgive me Annika. Will you marry me." He held the ring out to her. "Will you marry me."

Yes!! yes, I will marry you. She was smiling.

The next thing they heard were the happy screams of Jenna and Annika's mother. They were jumping and hugging each other.

He got up and kissed her so deeply and passionately.

"Thank you honey, I will never let you down. I love you so much. Thank you."

"You can stop screaming now girls." She showed them her ring. They all were beaming with smiles.

CHAPTER TWENTY-TWO

THE DAY OF the wedding came. Julia and Ms. Peggy were going over the site of the wedding making sure everything was done and done well. The fact that the wedding planners were doing an excellent had nothing to do with Julia.

Overlooking the turquoise waters of the Caribbean Sea, the wedding was set to take place on the cinnamon hill golf course. One hundred white chairs with blush colored cushions were set out all in perfect rows.

Why aren't the fans on the chairs yet, I need to see them out now."

"Yes Ms. Jervais." One of the planners ran to get the fans.

Ms. Peggy smiled at the planner. She wasn't as stern as Julia was.

At the alter there were two six foot tall columns that were daintily but not sparingly wrapped in roses of a delicate pink and very small whites. The fragrance that they gave off was heavenly. At the backdrop was a wall of flower all white roses so beautiful.

"Beautiful work." Ms. Peggy said to the florist.

"Thank you." The florist replied.

The women walked over to the aisle runner. White with gold trimmings. This entire area was concrete. It was covered with artificial grass so as to fit in with the lawn, the runner was perfectly placed over the grass. Julia will not have her future daughter in law walking down the aisle with grass and mud on her heels.

"They did a great job covering up the concrete."

"Yes, they sure did. I`ts beautiful." Ms. Peggy was so sincere in her reply. She was so happy for her daughter and Julia saw it all in her eyes. The ladies hugged each other for a moment.

We can't ruin our make up with tears.

"Haha no we can`t". Julia laughed.

It was a happy day.

"Where is our grandchild?" Ms. Peggy asked.

CHAPTER TWENTY-THREE

"**R**elax girl. Let the people do your make up."
"I am relaxed Jenna."

She was whitening her teeth with a laser system. Her hair was also being done at the same time as her makeup and she was a bit fidgety.

"You are very beautiful and easy to work with Annika." This came from the leader of the glam squad as Jenna had nicknamed them.

She smiled a thank you.

Eyebrows perfectly arched, make up so natural you would think she wasn't wearing any at all. She was glowing. She was stunning.

The hour was fast approaching. Guests were already milling in and that was the que for the dj to start playing music that had been chosen by the happy couple.

Inside the bridal suite the girls were getting dressed. The ladies in cream colored dresses and the bride in a blush toned dress. All sweetheart necklines.

"Jenna, thank you for being my friend all these years." "You have supported me through thick and thin. I love you sis."

"I love you too Annika, stop or else you are going to make us cry."

The ladies hugged each other." It`s time to marry your man girl."

Both mothers hugged Annika and Jenna. Theirs was a beautiful friendship.

The men were upstairs in the suite above where the ladies were. They were getting ready now. Fresh haircuts, Blue tailored suits, dark brown shoes, blush ties and pocket pieces. They looked dapper. Four groomsmen, and Malcolm. Michael Jervais` only son is getting married in a matter of minutes.

"Hey MJ, look at daddy all suited up for mommy" Michael was speaking to his grandson. He was so proud, and he loved this boy so much. MJ was beautiful, healthy and happy. He looked like both parents. He had his grandfather's hazel eyes. Michael and Julia loved their grandchild.

"Da da", the baby sounded. Malcolm kissed his son.

"Da da." He touched his father's face. Malcolm kissed his hand.

Let`s go boys, its time. Michael was directing them out of the suite." Lukie, you have the rings?"

"Yes sir."

"Dad, thank you for everything, I love you"

"I love you too son, and you too grandson."

Michael Jervais was very proud at this moment in his life. His son and grandson in the same room. Three generation of Jervais`.

The groomsmen were standing in place. Malcolm was shaking hands with the pastor. He knew Malcolm as a child. The family had come to church every Sunday. They still came but not so often. He was happy to see the young man making such a bold move.

All the friends and family were sitting in their seats. Everyone happy for the couple. The wedding song came on. Everyone turned around to see the beautiful bride walk down the aisle. She was a beauty to look at.

Malcolm`s heart was in his throat. The tears in his eyes welled up just a dam does with river water. Just to see her walking towards him. He had a flashback. All they have been through together, all he put her through and she still loved him enough to marry him. She deserved the world. He would give it to her. He truly loved her. The tears came, he couldn't hold it back. She truly was as pretty as a picture.

Annika was looking ahead of her, to the man she was going to spend the rest of her life with. The father of her child. She loved Malcolm with all her heart. She didn't think about the wrongs he had done. She was just thinking of the beautiful future they were going to have together. She truly believed that. Today was the first day of the rest of their lives and she was so looking forward to that. she didn't want to ruin her make up, but she was feeling so overwhelmed with it all. She smiled. He was so handsome. She thought he was crying but she couldn't tell for sure from under the veil.

She got the aisle. Her mother placed her hand in Malcolm's, she stepped back and sat in her seat. She didn't know she was crying until Julia started to dab at her face.

"They are so in love with each other. can you feel it or is it just me?"

"What they have is something truly beautiful." replied Julia.

CHAPTER TWENTY-FOUR

"**M**ichael Juinor, have some fruit."

She was on the phone with Malcolm.

"Say hi to daddy, he will be home soon."

"Hi daddy.?"

"Yes tiger, I`m coming home soon, ok"

"Ok daddy, love you."

"I love you more tiger."

"Ok Malcolm, I`ll see you soon honey."

He hung up. It has been two years since they have been married. Things were very good. He was a wonderful husband and a great father.

The more MJ grew, the more he looked like his father. His grandparents came by very regularly and always brought gifts. Overall, they were very happy and living a good life.

Annika stayed home with MJ. She didn't want a nanny raising her son. The decision to stay home and raise their son was very good in the eyes of Michael and Julia. They thought it spoke highly of Annika`s character.

Malcolm should have been home already. It was now two hours after the phone call. She had given her son a bath and he was now getting ready for bed.

"The little boy yawned, as Annika read; his mother knew that was a sign he was very tired."

"Tired mommy," said MJ

"Yes baby, that's the end of the story for tonight. You are tired."

She kissed his forehead "I love you Malcolm, goodnight."

He was already sleeping.

She tucked his blanket under his chin, turned on his nightlight and closed the door.

She went back downstairs to the kitchen. Her husband still wasn't home.

She picked up the phone to call him. She heard the key in the door. It was him.

'It's been three hours since you said you would be home. Your son was waiting for you. Where have you been?" She asked in hushed tones.

"I was out for a minute with the boys, didn't know I should ask your permission first."

"Shhhh. You'll wake the baby" she said.

He was drinking, she smelled it on his breath

"Tell me you didn't drive home."

"Who drove you home then."

"You said not to tell you." Malcom mocked her.

"You are being very careless and irresponsible Malcolm, goodnight."

She turned her back to walk away from him.

He grabbed her by the arm and swung her around. He kissed her lips with such force he bit her lip.

"You are my wife you will not walk away from me."

"Let me go Malcolm"

He raised her blouse and placed his palms over her breast.

"Come do your wifely duties."

This happened twice already when he was drunk. He was drunk now.

"Malcolm stop" she slapped his face.

That only seem to arouse him more.

He pulled her to the dining table which was bare except for a centerpiece.

He shoved her on top of the table. She tried to get away from him, but she was no match for him.

He started sucking her exposed breast while he stroked the other one roughly.

"You are so hot, you turn me on."

"Malcolm not like this." she resisted.

He got on top of her, he was kissing and sucking every exposed part of her upper body.

He pulled her boy shorts off with one hand while the other held her wrists.

She tried wriggling away from him. No use.

She didn't realize that he had got his pants down. He spread her legs and forced his penis inside her. She was crying now.

"Malcolm please don't." she didn't want to wake the baby up. She was more concerned about MJ.

"Honey, not like this, you don't have to rush."

He wasn't slowing down, and he wasn't stopping.

"I love you, what more do you want?"

Malcolm was talking at her

"You have the house, the car, the accounts what's the problem all I want to do is fuck my wife when I want to fuck my wife."

He was picking up the tempo now why are you being so fucking cold. "Don't you know that you are my world."

He started kissing her lips again. He bit her neck. He was about to climax. He held on to her hair.

"You are hurting me Malcolm."

He didn't hear, he didn't care he began thrusting even harder.

She was crying by this. He pulled out and ejaculated on her tummy.

He kissed her again.

"I love you," he gave her a wicked smile, got up and staggered upstairs.

She used her blouse to clean herself up. She got up and walked to the stairs. She was in so much pain. She was crying.

"Why is this happening to me?" She asked herself over and over again.

She dragged herself up the stairs and to M J's room. He was fast asleep. He looked like an angel.

She went to the bedroom. He was sprawled in the sofa beside the bed. She went to the bathroom and started the Jacuzzi tub.

She filled it with water, as hot as she could handle it, added bath salts and just laid in there.

She was depressed. She didn't know what to do. You aren't supposed to talk about your married life to anyone. She was dealing with a lot. This was a lot. She had stopped crying and started putting plans together in her head. She was in the tub until the water got cold. She got out and dried herself off.

She rubbed lotion over her skin, moisturizer on her face and she slipped into her teddy and went to bed. She didn't even look at Malcolm. That night she dreamt of life far away from where she was. A life that was happy and fulfilling. A life of love. She didn't see Malcolm in that dream. not even once.

At some point in the night he got up and went to bed. He was still dressed in his suit. He had a terrible headache. He got up again to get some aspirin in the bathroom. Annika was in here. It smelled like her. Suddenly his memories of what happened came flooding back to him.

"O my God no!"

He instantly knew what he did. It happened every time he drank. He had stopped cheating and began drinking but he could not hold his own when he drank. How the hell did he expect to just act like everything was alright when he knew what he had done. Drunk or not, there was no excuse.

He showered, got dressed and went to bed. He hugged her. She pulled away. He couldn't blame her.

"Annika, darling, I'm sorry. I don't know what is happening to me: Please Annika. I am so sorry forgive me."

She did not stir.

He was in deep shit.

"She won't speak to me now"

She always becomes silent when she is upset.

"I need to find a way to make her understand that it's not me, I'm not myself when these things happen." He was thinking to himself.

"I am so sorry Annika." Sleep eluded him for the rest of the night.

He was beside himself with shame. She could file charges. Not that he thought she would but who knows. It was all his doing and he had to face the consequences.

He was going down a dark path. He needed to get his act together once and for all.

CHAPTER TWENTY-FIVE

SINCE THAT LAST episode with Malcolm. Nothing had changed. Things had actually gotten worse. The verbal abuse had started. In an attempt to fix her marriage, she had begun reading books, listening to motivational marriage counselors.

When it seemed, all hope was lost she decided to speak to Malcolm's mother. Julia.

Turns out that opened a whole other can of worms. Julia had made it known to her that she knew she would come to her at one point or the other. Michael was just the same, but Julia refused to leave her marriage and a s a result Malcolm grew up seeing all that and as destiny would have it. He became his father's son.

"You cannot leave your marriage, it is your duty as a wife to see it through. No matter what. He is already your husband."

"I am very sorry Julia, I am not happy. I can't do that."

Annika knew then what she had to do, and she would do it.

That evening Annika made sure that herself and Malcolm would have a beautiful intimate evening. Mj was at his grandparent's house. No doubt he was being spoilt.

She prepared a beautiful meal of yellow fin bass, Pilaf rice and kale. Malcolm's favorite. She had decided to stop at an adult novelty ty store and bought a beautiful lingerie set. Afterall, Malcolm had seen her in all the ones she had, and she had a lot. Malcolm would be made to feel like a king tonight. She would make sure of it.

"The table is set, everything is in place, time to go shower" She said to herself.

She went upstairs to the bathroom and decided to run a bath instead.

"Malcolm wouldn't be home until around seven." She had three hours.

She poured a very satisfying amount of bath gel.

"Yes, exactly how I want it, not too hot, not too cold." She was going to lay in that tub until the water got cold. A little over an hour later she was just getting out. She dabbed her skin dry.

She moisturized her body slowly, she then applied her favorite scent Japanese cherry blossom. She sat her vanity making herself even more beautiful, which she didn't need to do. She applied matte stain to her lips, mascara to finish up

"Perfect" she said as she smacked her lips.

She slipped into her lingerie.

Wow, this sure is soft. She examined herself in the full-length mirror which was actually a wall of mirrors.

The lace took to her figure, softly falling over her breast, flat at her stomach and spilling over her hips. It was crotch less and there was a bow just above her ass., she slid the stockings up her thighs. She fastened the clasp that connected them to the lingerie. She was hot

"Now, do I wear red or black heels she decided to wear black, at least it matched perfectly, she put on a light soft black dress that stopped just above her knees.

She called Malcolm.

"How are you love?"

"I'm good honey."

"Will you be home soon"

"Sure, in about 40 minutes."

"Ok honey, just checking. I love you."

She replaced the receiver.

"Hmm Malcolm smirked, sounds like she is in high spirits." He smiled.

Annika used the opportunity to double check the food, the table, herself.

"Shit the wine!" She exclaimed.

She hurried to the bar to see if there was a suitable white wine. She settled for Chenin Blanc, picked up the ice bucket and proceeded to put the wine on ice. she set it on the table

"Now everything is perfect." She smiled as a million thoughts ran through her head.

She patiently waited for her husband.

She didn't have to wait long. Less than ten minutes later he was turning his key in the lock.

She met him at the door, took his iPad, his keys and iPhone. She undid his tie. She kissed his lips softly and sensually.

"How was your day honey?". She kissed him again.

"I'm so glad you are home, I missed you today baby."

He started to reply but she placed a finger over his lips.

"Go upstairs, shower, get dressed and come back to me baby, tonight it`s all about you.

She kissed him on the lips and let her manicured fingers trail down to rest below his Gucci belt. He was rock hard.

"I love you."

"Shhh." She whispered.

She guided him to the stairs. He obediently went up the stairs. He did as he was instructed.

All the while thinking, "Did I forget her birthday, is it our anniversary?"

By the time he came back down she had dinner plated. wine was being poured as he walked over to where she was. she smelled good, always put herself together in a manner that he loved. None of his side pieces could hold a candle to his wife.

"Wow, when did you do all this, everything looks so awesome." He was still turning over in his mind. "What did she find out".

He was wearing the clothes she set out for him. White linen suit, Yves saint Laurent and matching slippers.

You look so handsome honey she took his hand and led him to the chair at the head of the table. She opened his napkin and tucked it into his collar. She sat in his lap. She kissed his lips, his neck and nibbled on his ears.

"Is everything ok with us babe?"

His right arm came up to touch her face. She got up and sat in the chair beside him.

"Eat" she motioned to him.

"Yes, everything is ok, I just wanted to show you that you are special to me and I do love you darling".

"You are such an amazing wife, thank you."

"Anything for you my darling."

"Everything tastes so good honey, I'm amazed."

"Just as you like it babe."

"Let me get that plate for you honey, she got up, sit back and relax honey, you work so hard for us let me take care of you."

He watched her as she removed the plates and brought them to the sink

"No one will be doing dishes tonight, that is for sure". He licked his lips.

She was always good to him, but he couldn't shake the feeling that something was up., but he decided to relax and enjoy his wife. She came back with the entree.

"O honey, is this bass? wow smells awesome."

"I know It's your favorite, hope you enjoy." She poured him another glass of wine.

She made small portions but they were just enough to hit the spot. Malcolm enjoyed his meal. He truly was feeling like a king.

When he was finished he held her palm in his.

"That was awesome baby, you sure went overboard this time."

"No honey, I'm just getting started."

He downed his glass of wine in one swig.

"She walked over to him. she sat on his lap

"Did you truly enjoy everything love?"

"Oh darling, I sure did. Everything was beautiful. Thank you."

She hugged him, not forgetting what this dinner was about. She closed her eyes.

He lifted her chin. He kissed her lips

She stood up. Reached for her zipper which went all the way down the front of the dress. She let it fall to the ground.

Malcolm gasped. He had to catch his breath...

She pulled the hairpin and let her Brazilian extensions fall all the way down to her ass. She straddled her husband right there at the dining table he was speechless. Who was this woman. He loved it. He has always wanted his wife to always show wanton abandonment when they made love but wow.

This was kicking it up a few notches. Dominating him. She had him where she wanted him. She was kissing him deeply. Her tongue dancing with his. Her full breast teasing his chest. He cupped her breast with his hand and kissed and sucked on her nipple. That made her go wild and he knew it. He got up with her still wrapped around his waist. He laid her on the table and slowly unwrapped her legs from around him. He held them upright, then slowly spread them. He kissed her face, he kissed her belly button. He placed his lips on her clitoris. She shuddered under his body. He kissed her lightly. He flicked his tongue.

Ahhh…she moaned. He let his tongue roam her vagina freely. So fresh. Her pussy tasted like water and he always told her so. He enjoyed eating her out. just the thoughts in his mind made his cock even harder.

He dived in with his tongue, so warm and wet, he was sucking and kissing her with a passion that you could feel. She was actually pushing his head down. She wanted more and more.

He loved when she did that. He knew he had her then. He was writhing under his mouth, arching her hip upwards. She was going to climax, and he wasn't having it. He flipped her over so fast that she was a bit surprised.

He now had her ass in the air and she was already wet, he mounted her, dropped his pants and entered her a bit roughly. She cried out, she had climaxed, but Malcolm didn't ease the pressure. He was grinding inside her, she felt so good. He was plunging in and out of her, he could feel all of her. He was now coming to his own climax. He grabbed her hair. He was whispering to her now.

"you are mine, remember that, my wife. I love you so much. I love you Annika. No one can take your place, no matter what I love you."

He shuddered, kissing her. He spilled his seed inside he warmth. His mind was whirling. She kissed his face, neck. She looked him in the eyes.

"I really do love you Malcolm", her body shook with intense pleasure.

He wasn't done with her yet. Even though he just climaxed, he was as hard a s a flagpole in winter. He lifted her almost limp body onto his shoulders. He was tormenting her with her sweetness with his tongue.

He squeezed her ass cheeks, she was moaning while his tongue kept up a romantic dance with her clit. she climaxed again. Malcolm slowly let her down onto the floor she stood there all sexy and all his. He kissed her breasts, one after the other he circled her nipples with his tongue, gently nibbling on them with his teeth. They were both sweating now, albeit the air turned on to seventy-four degrees.

"Do you like that babe?"

"Honey!" she gasped

She stepped back from Malcolm and knelt in front of him. She kissed his pelvic bones. It was always a tickle spot for him. She licked the tip of his manhood. Her tongue was playing games with his family jewels. He panted.

"Darling, put it in your mouth."

She pretended to oblige him, only to slide her tongue down his shaft. She would when she was ready. She licked her way slowly back to the erect tip, she could feel him throbbing. She passed her wet tongue over his mushroom., without warning she took him entirely into her warm mouth.

"Agghhhh!" he let out. "You are so good mmmm"

She was like a soft vacuum, in and out he went. She was making him crazy he was grabbing onto the nearby dining table, he was weak, he placed both hands at the sides of her head. Pulling her towards him.

She knew he was about to climax, she upped the tempo.

"Babe! I`m about to cum." he screamed.

She didn't stop.

He shuddered.

She felt his every throb. He fell to his knees.

She smiled.

She got up and left him there on the carpet. He had to get his wits about him.

She went up the stairs, rinsed her mouth and brushed her teeth. She then showered. All the while going over in her head the plans she had set in motion. One thing she knew for sure is that she loved her husband she began to cry. Her tears mingled with the water from the showerhead.

After a lovemaking session like this, how could she leave.

Malcolm opened the door, he sensed something was off. But didn't make an issue of it.

"Wow! Honey, what got into you?" That was awesome.

Before he could say another word

"Malcolm, I`m leaving you."

The winds were knocked from his sails.

"What!?, I don't understand."

"It's over Malcolm, I refuse to be second best to your whores and your drink, we have had these conversations over and over again and I refuse to be treated the way you treat me. I`m done."

"Annika, are you kidding me right now? I don't know what you are going on about. Didn't we just make love, how…"

"Yes we did, that was the final time. I`ll send the papers for you to sign in the mail."

All the time she was talking she was getting dressed. She had on white jeans and a black polo shirt. Nothing fancy but she looked hot in anything she donned. She put on her black and white converse sneakers. Studs in her ears. She had slipped the wedding band off her finger and laid it on the dressing table in her bedroom. She looked a picture.

"Honey, I love you. Don't do this. What about all we`ve been through, our son?"

She shot him a wicked glance.

"Don't you dare bring our baby into this, were you thinking about us when you were fucking around with everything that wore a skirt. She was shouting now. How dare you?"

Malcolm was silent. She was right.

He knew in the back of his mind this day would come but he had convinced himself that she would always forgive him. Seemed his luck had run out.

She grabbed her tote and headed for the door. She had already packed clothes and essentials in the car.

"Annika please, don't leave me."

She slammed the door behind her.

He stood frozen in space. He knew she was serious. She was gone.

He heard her car drive off. He had no idea where she was going, and he had no one to blame but himself.

CHAPTER TWENTY-SIX

MALCOLM POURED HIMSELF a glass of Jack Daniels. He sat in the same chair at the same table where him and his wife made beautiful love. Now she was gone, and he was all alone.

"My son. Where is my son?"

He tried calling Annika to see if she would pick up. She didn't.

He called his parents.

"Is Annika and MJ there?"

His mother answered.

"No Malcolm, she was here earlier but they left. What is going on over there?"

"Damn it", he shouted.

"She left me mom, she left me and took our son." He was sobbing now.

"Malcolm, you've been drinking."

He didn't respond, he didn't have to.

His father's voice came over the line.

"Malcolm, I thought you were smarter than this, have you not learned from my mistakes. This is on you."

He knew what his dad was saying was the truth. He didn't argue. Annika was gone.

CHAPTER TWENTY-SEVEN

AT THE SANGSTER'S International Airport, Annika and her son boarded a flight to Miami. Her friend Annika had migrated to the U.S. and they were both still very much in touch. In less than two hours, the friends were reunited.

"A who dat screeched Jenna!". She had left Jamaica not long after her friend's wedding.

"Jenna, I`m so happy to see you."

The friends embraced.

Jenna`s focus went on the baby boy. "MJ you are so handsome like your grandpa."

she squealed. She took the baby from Annika and they walked to her car parked not too far away.

"Jenna, thank you so much for taking me in, I don't know what I would do without you."

'Annika please, you know I love you girl", just try not to think too much.'

They got to her Range Rover.

Annika put the car seat in the back and Jenna strapped MJ in.

The two friends were talking, having animated conversations. Soon they go to the condo.

She pulled into the garage, they all got into the elevator.

"Jenna, what is this?"

Jenna had gotten supplies, clothes and everything she thought baby MJ would want. They would shop for Annika tomorrow.

"What is what she laughed."

Annika cried and they embraced again.

While Annika took a bath, Jenna fed MJ and put him to bed in a nice crib she had bought for him. She was a proud godmother. She loved her friend and she loved her godson. She knew how Malcolm was, thing is, Annika had known too but she thought she could change him. Typical mistake women make. She wouldn't judge her friend though. As far as she was concerned it didn't matter. She had never been one to settle with any man and she doubted that very much.

Annika emerged from the bathroom a few minutes later. When she saw that the baby was asleep, she started to cry, it was too much. Jenna just hugged her friend. She never said a word.

"Thank you so much Jenna."

"No need pretty girl, no need, you need to get some rest. Go to bed," "We will talk in the morning."

Annika went to her room. She climbed between the cool white sheets. They smelt so good. She laid there silently thinking.

"Did I do the right thing, my mom, what is she thinking right now?"

It will not be a walk in the park, but she was strong, she would be alright.

"No. I have to think about my son and myself first. I refuse to be a victim." "This is the beginning of a new day, a new life". "My happiness is up to me. The old Annika is no more." Life would be what she wanted it to be. It was time for her to take back her life into her hands.

She drifted off to sleep sometime around three am. As she slept that night, her phone was vibrating in her bag. She never heard it. She was getting messages through her social media, her voicemail as well. She was never aware of it though

She was at peace. That night she slept as soundly as a new born baby. She dreamt of white sandy beaches, herself and MJ walking along the shore, picking up seashells. Her son was laughing, and she was happy. She was truly at peace.

But it wasn't to be.

"Daddy" MJ was saying.

Daddy is not here now sweetheart, come to mommy."

"Want daddy...."

"Where is daddy MJ?" Jenna chimed in.

The boy went to his mommy and hugged her. He was saying something unintelligible.

"Yuh feisty like, who yuh arguing with?" Jenna jeered.

"Jenna leave MJ alone. Annika laughed.

Annika began looking around her.

"Have you seen my phone Jenna?"

"No maam."

She handed MJ to Jenna and went to check her bag for the phone.

"You are so cute, what a handsome boy you are?", she kissed his cheeks. MJ smiled a gummy smile at her.

Annika was looking on the bed and in the bathroom, she remembered that she never took it from her bag. She found it there. The battery was at ten percent.

"Ten missed calls, six voicemails?" she mouthed. Her heart sank to the sole of her feet.

Did she think Malcolm would just let her go like that?

He had been calling her all through the night into the early morning hours. Malcolm would not give up. He could find her if he wanted to.

"He has all kinds of connections, what am I going to do now." She thought to herself.

The good thing is that Malcolm didn't knew where Jenna lived. He had just assumed she went back to England, so she had that working for her.

CHAPTER TWENTY-EIGHT

JENNA HAD GOTTEN her a job as an HR administrator at a high-profile hotel in Miami. Jenna worked in the same hotel and luckily, they provide daycare services on the first floor of the building.

It had worked out so well, thanks to Jenna.

"I will begin working next Monday so at least I'll have an income coming in so money will not be an issue."

Afterall, she did have money in the bank. Malcolm had made sure she was set.

She began listening to the voicemails he had left on her phone.

"Annika! where are you, where is MJ. I don't know what I did to make you leave me in such a manner. My darling. Please, we can talk things through. Just come home baby. Please. I need you, I love you."

Next message....

"Annika, where are you? Come home. Why are you doing this to me. Why are you being like this. Don't you know I love you?"

He was getting hysterical, she knew he was drinking. Next message....

"Annika, if you don't bring my child back to me by midday tomorrow you will be wanted by the police for kidnapping. I know people don't you forget that. You hear me. Leave if you want but you will never have my son!"

Wow, he was flying off the handle. He was pissed.

Next message....

"Baby, I love you. come home. I promise I'll be better, please believe me this time. I will do better to be a great husband to you honey: You are a great wife and you deserve to be happy. I will see a therapist honey. I will be the man you want. Please come home baby. I miss you."

Jenna was standing in the doorway, she heard the messages.

"So wah yuh go do now?"

Startled, Annika turned around to see her friend concerned eyes and her baby's smiling face. She knew what she had to do, it wasn't going to be easy.

"Jenna, I don't want to keep Michael from his father."

"Are you trying to convince me or yourself?"

"What do you mean by that?"

"Yuh can fool anybody you want but not me, me know yuh better than yuh know yuhself."

Annika shook her head and walked over to take the baby. She was deep in thought. She knew she made the right choice in leaving, as much as it hurt her: she knew she deserved better and that was her decision.

CHAPTER TWENTY-NINE

HER MOTHER HAD tried her best to convince her to stay in her marriage no matter what, because that's what you did. They had a difference in opinion and it led to an argument. Annika had made it clear to her mother that she wasn't her and she would not stay in a marriage that she wasn't happy in.

"Annika, you made vows in front of God and man."

"Ok, I shouldn't want to be happy, I shouldn't want a good life for my son, I should be just like you a settle for what I can get."

"You need to fight for your marriage child."

"Fight, what do you know about fighting? you never fought for one thing in your life. Maybe if you fought I wouldn't be in this situation."

She moved the baby to the other hip.

"How dare you, do you know anything? Do you know what it means to be fourteen and pregnant, to be at the mercies of a man you thought loved you because you were never love by you parents; to be beaten because you weren't taught to cook, wash or clean; You have no idea what I endured to make sure your life was just a bit better than mine; you were cooking, cleaning washing and doing everything at age twelve, so don't you dare speak to me like that ever again."

Annika felt ashamed. "I'm very sorry, I shouldn't have said that."

Ms. Peggy hugged her daughter. "Don't ever apologize for what you feel my love, we don't always understand the choices of others. I love you girl. I'm sorry too."

Ms. Peggy kissed her grandson. He reached for his grandmother.

Annika handed him to her. She hugged the baby and he looked at her with eyes that seemed to know the secrets of life. MJ smiled.

"Grandma loves you Michael."

Annika hugged her mother amid the tears.

"I love you mommy and I will keep in touch, I promise."

They all walked to the car.

"Be safe my child and take care of MJ you are a mother now and I know you will do everything for your child. I love you."

Annika put the car in drive.

"Goodbye mom."

Ms. Peggy waved as her daughter and grandchild drove away. She went inside and started to pray for her daughter.

CHAPTER THIRTY

ANNIKA WAS SAD. She missed her mother. She didn't get the chance to feel sorry for herself long as her phone was vibrating. It was Julia.

"How are you doing darling? Jules asked as she answered the phone."

"I`m doing very well thank you. MJ is well also."

"I`m just calling to check in with you love. I know this can't be easy for you and I totally understand your situation, as mothers we have to do what is right for our children; it's just a pity I learnt that lesson too late."

"It`s alright Jules, it`s not your fault. Malcolm is a grown man who has a choice of what he chooses to do and not to do. He made his choice, you are a wonderful mother, Remember that."

"Thank you for saying that my dear, you are such a lovely girl. I won't keep you too long, kiss my grand baby for me and please, if there is anything you need I`m just a phone call away. I love you Annika do take care, ok love."

"Yes Julia, I will and thank you very much."

With that, Julia hung up.

CHAPTER THIRTY-ONE

"You know where she is!"

She turned around to see Malcolm glaring at her.

"How long have you been standing there?"

"Long enough to know that you know where my family is, but you just want me to suffer." He huffed and puffed.

"Shut up with your foolishness. That's what you do. Blame everyone else for the dumb decisions you make. She is a great wife and a wonderful mother but no, just like your father; You have to go chasing every skirt in town. At least she has the good sense to do what I was afraid to do."

"Get away from me boy and don't ask me a damn thing, you should be ashamed."

With that, Julia walked right past him. She was very upset.

Malcolm knew his mother was right. He made the mess he was in and he was the one who had to fix it.

Why was it so hard to stay true to his wife? she was everything he needed. Beautiful, smart, loyal, sexy and she was the most amazing mother but no, He had to be on the prowl and the drinking didn't make it easier either.

He was headed down a collision course and he had to get help.

CHAPTER THIRTY-TWO

ANNIKA DIDN'T DWELL too long on the phone call. She was encouraged by it though. She had given her mother- in – law the number just in case.

"O well." she thought.

Jenna came home a few minutes after the call from Malcolm, bubbly and excited as usual after her workout. With coffee in her hands.

"One for you."

"Aww thanks love, how was the gym today?"

"Fun as usual." she mocked curtsy.

She walked over to where the baby was, all comfy on the plush carpet watching Leapfrog ABC's.

"Give aunty a kiss, muah"

The baby laughed. MJ was a happy baby, never fussy and Jenna truly loved him.

"So, I just got off the phone with Malcolm"

"A lie, wah him say?"

"He wants to see me, he misses me and MJ".

"And you miss your sexy husband." Jenna made a kissy face.

CHAPTER THIRTY-THREE

A DAY LATER MALCOLM arrived at the south beach restaurant twenty minutes earlier than scheduled. He ordered a sweetened tea.

He was excited and anxious. He wanted to see his family.

He was there with his heart on his sleeves. He had no idea what would happen, but he had to try.

She had called him back late in the evening and asked how soon he could be in Miami. They spoke for a few hours about all that happened and how to go about saving their marriage. It was a very soulful conversation. Very deep.

He had showered as fast as he could and called Lukie to take him to the airport.

He bought a first-class ticket on JetBlue. He had found a hotel online and checked in. He felt like the richest man in Babylon.

A white Range Rover pulled in to the parking lot. Annika got out, walked to the back of the car and unlocked the child seat before she could finish, Malcolm was there assisting her.

"I saw you pull in I couldn't wait, I`m sorry."

They both smiled at each other.

"Hi.", smiled Annika

"Hi."

His heart was in his mouth.

"You look so good Annika."

"Thank you."

Malcolm reached in the car and lifted his son out.

It felt like forever. He hasn't seen his son in months and he could feel his heart melting. It was as if he was just born.

"Michael, daddy missed you so much, did you miss daddy".

MJ hugged his daddy and wouldn't let go off his neck.

Malcolm was over the moon. He kissed his little boy.

He hugged Annika. She hugged him back.

"I have to admit, I sure missed being hugged by you." Said Annika.

"You don't know how crazy I've been without you both. I love you Annika."

He took he hand and gently led her to the restaurant, MJ riding on his neck. This is what heaven felt like.

Malcolm had tears in his eyes. To the outside world, they were the perfect family.

He led them to a table.

"You have been in Miami all this time and my mother knew and didn't tell me." He said out loud.

"I bet she knows exactly where too; he didn't know how this would turn out, but he was going to do his best to get his family back home where they belong.

CHAPTER THIRTY- FOUR

THE CONVERSATION INSIDE the restaurant went well.

"Sweetie, I`m glad we had a chance to talk."

"Yes." She answered Malcolm. "It was, we really needed this."

They hugged and smiled at each other.

MJ was fast asleep. Malcom lifted him out of the seat and held him to his chest. They walked back to the car. He strapped his son in his car seat. Annika stood by the door.

"MJ is growing up so fast, pretty soon we will be playing football and fishing together." Malcolm stated.

"Yes, you are absolutely right but I don't see him fishing." She laughed.

"What?" he feigned shock.

"It`s a Jervais tradition, he has to fish."

They both laughed.

"On a more serious note though honey, I truly have seen the errors of my ways. Both mom and dad have been helping me through the twelve-step program. I am doing awesome now and I think it's time you guys came home. I know and understand that where we are today being as a result of my stupidity: and I want you to know that I regret it all. I truly am sorry for all the hurt and pain I caused you, us our family. I love you Annika."

"I do trust that you have learnt your lessons Malcolm: I refuse to spend my life making excuses for you and stifle my own happiness and that of our son Love, marriage is serious business. We just can't go back to the way things were before. I hope you know that." She stared him in the eyes.

"You won't my love, you have my word."

"Hm mmm" She smarted.

"I have to get going now." She got in the car.

"Ok honey, drive safely." He leaned in the window and gave her a kiss on the lips.

"I love you and I can't wait for us to get back to our lives."

"Me too Malcolm, take care of yourself"

She waved at him. He blew her a kiss while she drove off.

He couldn't stand watching her drive away from him. Really, it was like losing her and his son again.

It's just for a while she will be home soon, He reasoned.

CHAPTER THIRTY- FIVE

ANNIKA WAS LOOKING in her rearview mirror through watery eyes. She loved Malcolm with all she had. She loved her son even more. Was she doing the right thing in taking back Malcom. She trusted that he was really changed this time. Aftercall, his parents were helping him every step of the way to get over this addiction.

MJ stirred in his car seat.

"Daddy"

"You will see daddy very soon baby. He had to go back to work."

"Ok mommy." He went back to sleep.

Annika laughed to herself. He woke up just to ask for daddy. O lord. She thought about all that transpired and how it affected everyone.

"Yes. I am making the right decision." She reasoned.

She would leave for Jamaica the day after tomorrow.

At this very minute, Jenna and Malcolm was planning a surprise party for Annika and MJ. He missed them so much and he just wanted everything to go right for once. Jenna was his go to person.

The friendship that the girls had was unbreakable. You would think they were sisters and not friends but then again: once you've been friends that long you became family. So, his mother said.

CHAPTER THIRTY -SIX

IT WAS 2:45 pm in Jamaica. The flight had been very comfortable. They stepped out the gate and she put MJ down to walk.

"Daddy, daddy!"

Mj screamed and ran off as fast as his little legs would carry him.

Annika hadn't tried to stop him. At the end of the gate stood the Jervais clan and Jenna. Who said she had a business meeting and wouldn't be there to see her off at the airport.

Ms Peggy was behind Malcolm hiding. It was part of their plan. Trouble is she couldn't deal with the suspense. She dashed from behind him to hug her daughter. She started screaming.

Annika herd her scream before she saw her mom. She dashed to meet her both women laughing and hugging like kids in the airport.

"I missed you so much mommy."

"Annika, o Annika my girl, I missed you every day." She was crying tears of joy now.

"Mommy stop crying." they hugged for what seemed an eternity.

"What about us? Malcolm's dad said

They all laughed.

Jervais senior gave her a large bouquet of lilies and an even bigger hug.

"Welcome home Annika. We sure missed you."

"I missed you all too."

Next was Jules. She kissed Annika on both cheeks.

"Darling, welcome back, we have a lot of catching up to do."

"Thank you for everything Julia."

Hello, its my turn. Piped Malcolm, she is my wife. They laughed at that.

He kissed Annika.

"Hello my love. Its so good to be holding you again. I won't ever let you out of my sight again: I love you so much."

"I love you too Malcolm."

They kissed and hugged while the others looked on. It was wonderful seeing these lovers together again.

"Mommy, daddy let's go!" shouted MJ who was being held by Jenna.

And you Jenna, said Annika. They both burst out laughing.

"I know I can be very convincing right."

She laughed and hugged her friend.

"I love you girl."

"I love you too Jenna."

Just then a familiar voice said

"Please don t go leave again, Malcolm is a total idiot without you."

"Lukie! Hey how are you doing?"

"Good now that you are back I won't need to babysit anymore. I can focus on important things." He smiled at Jenna who in turn hissed her teeth.

At that everyone laughed.

"Let's go."

EPILOGUE

ANNIKA AND MALCOLM laid in bed cuddling, talking, laughing and making plans.

MJ was with his grandparent's tonight's thought the couple needed some time by themselves.

"Thank you for the party honey, I never expected such a lavish welcome."

"Good, I'm just happy you are home."

He kissed her head.

She looked up at him.

"I love you."

She pulled his head down and kissed his lips.

He kissed her face, her eyes, her lips.

"I love you my wife, I love everything about you."

The Jervais's made love until they were both spent.

Life as Annika knew it was back on track. She loved her family, she loved her husband. They both had a bright and wonderful future ahead of them.

He had loved her enough to come after her and that said a lot.

"Thank you, Lord, for all your blessings."

Annika prayed silently. She couldn't stop the tears of joy flowing down her beautiful face. She was truly happy.

Malcom didn't want to take his hand from off his wife. He loved her with all he was. He messed up, but God gave him a second chance, with which he would prove that he was worthy to be her husband and a father to their son.

He would never give her cause to question his love ever again. He had learned his lesson. He wouldn't blow it this time. In life you got as good as you gave, Afterall it's just life… nothing personal.

ABOUT THE AUTHOR

MONIQUE GREW UP in Montego Bay Jamaica along with her mother and two siblings. With a simple childhood, one had to find ways to entertain themselves and her way was to read. She would read everything that had writing on it. Books made her happy.

She pursued vocational training after high school with qualifications that landed her a job at a high-end hotel in the Rose Hall, which is customary for young people on the Island who couldn't afford college. After some years of saving, she went on to pursue her bachelor's in education while being a waitress which was no easy fete. At the completion of her studies, she migrated to The United States of America where she presently resides with her son and husband.